E
pi $13.95
            Pinkwater, Daniel
            The phantom of
            the lunch wagon

DATE DUE

JA 21'9	AG 0 6		
FE 8'93			
MY 29'93			
JUL 19 95			
DEC 3 0 95			
MAR 1 1 96			
MAY 2 2 96			
OCT 07 96			
JUL 23			
OC 21 02			
AP 26 07			
3 0	8		

THE PHANTOM OF THE LUNCH WAGON

written and illustrated by DANIEL PINKWATER

Macmillan Publishing Company   New York   Maxwell Macmillan Canada   Toronto

Maxwell Macmillan International   New York Oxford Singapore Sydney

Macmillan Publishing Company is part of the Maxwell Communication
Group of Companies.
Macmillan Publishing Company
866 Third Avenue
New York, NY 10022
Maxwell Macmillan Canada, Inc.
1200 Eglinton Avenue East
Suite 200
Don Mills, Ontario M3C 3N1
First edition
Printed in the United States of America
10 9 8 7 6 5 4 3 2 1
The text of this book is set in 13 pt Clearface.
The illustrations are rendered in pen and ink with color markers.

Library of Congress Cataloging-in-Publication Data
Pinkwater, Daniel Manus.
The phantom of the lunch wagon / written and illustrated by Daniel
Pinkwater. – 1st ed.
p.   cm.
Summary: Chris Kevin-Keith fixes up and reopens an abandoned lunch
wagon, unaware that it originally closed because it was haunted by a
scary phantom.
ISBN 0-02-774641-0
[1. Restaurants, lunch rooms, etc.–Fiction. 2 Ghosts–Fiction.] I.Title
PZ7.P6335Ph 1992   [E]–dc20   92-3051

FOR JILL, OF COURSE

West Cheddar Street is in the part of town with all the shops. Everything is clean and bright. The buildings have fresh coats of paint. The shop windows are washed every week. The sidewalks are swept twice a day. There are banks and office buildings with brass nameplates polished like mirrors. Everything is shiny, and seems brand-new.

Except the old lunch wagon. It has been closed for many years. Once it was a real streetcar that ran on rails down the middle of West Cheddar Street.

Then it was lifted onto a foundation, and turned into a place that served food. A lunch wagon it was called. People would sit on stools facing a long counter. They would eat lunch, also breakfast, also supper. It was open all night and all day. A sign outside said, GUS'S: WE NEVER CLOSE.

But it did close. The windows got so dirty that no one could see inside. The paint peeled off. Weeds grew all around, and little trees grew out of the roof. Someone had nailed boards over the front door.

Few people remembered when Gus's Lunch Wagon had served hamburgers and tuna fish sandwiches and pieces of pie to the people who worked and shopped and lived around West Cheddar Street. Nobody remembered and nobody wondered why the lunch wagon had closed so long ago, and why it had been allowed to get so old and empty and dark.

Nobody remembered and nobody wondered—except Mr. Wiggers. Mr. Wiggers was old. He had seen everything, and he remembered everything.

"I remember Gus's Lunch Wagon in the old days," Mr. Wiggers would say. "And I remember when it closed, and why. I know why the old lunch wagon was allowed to get so dusty and empty and dark. I remember—but nobody listens to old Mr. Wiggers."

Chris Kevin-Keith came along. Chris Kevin-Keith loved lunch wagons and also diners, which are bigger restaurants that look like old railroad cars. When Chris Kevin-Keith saw the dusty, dark, and dirty old lunch wagon, he did not see something unloved and broken-down. "What a beautiful lunch wagon!" Chris Kevin-Keith said. "It's one of the best I've ever seen!"

Chris Kevin-Keith went to the City Hall. He went to the Hall of Records. "Who is the owner of the old lunch wagon?" he asked.

"Nobody knows," said the Hall of Records lady. "Nobody has paid taxes on it since 1952. You may buy it for a dollar, if you promise to tear it down and take it away."

"May I buy it for a dollar if I promise to fix it up?" Chris Kevin-Keith asked.

"Fix it up?" the Hall of Records lady asked. "Why would anyone want to do that?"

Chris Kevin-Keith bought the old lunch wagon for a dollar. The next day he went to work, clearing away the weeds and pulling up the little trees that were growing out of the roof.

Old Mr. Wiggers came along. "Going to tear it down and take it away?" Mr. Wiggers asked.

"Nope. Fixing it up," Chris Kevin-Keith said.

"Might be better to tear it down," old Mr. Wiggers said. "Might be better to tear it down and take it away, and scatter the pieces in all directions."

"Never!" Chris Kevin-Keith said. "This beautiful old lunch wagon will be beautiful again."

"Suit yourself," Mr. Wiggers said.

"Why do you say that?" Chris Kevin-Keith asked. "Do you know something I ought to know?"

"It doesn't matter what I know," old Mr. Wiggers said. "Nobody listens to me. Nobody listens to old Mr. Wiggers."

"I'm listening," Chris Kevin-Keith said. "What do you know about this old lunch wagon?"

"It's no use," old Mr. Wiggers said, walking away slowly. "Everybody ignores old Mr. Wiggers."

Old Mr. Wiggers was a little deaf as well as old and boring. He had not heard Chris Kevin-Keith say that he was interested in hearing what old Mr. Wiggers knew about the lunch wagon.

What old Mr. Wiggers knew about the lunch wagon was something frightening, scary, terrible, and awful. He knew why Gus, the first owner of the lunch wagon, had run away, never to return, why no one else had wanted to take over the lunch wagon, why it had been boarded up and neglected for so many years.

Old Mr. Wiggers knew that the lunch wagon had the worst thing a lunch wagon can have—the worst thing any house or shop, or post office or opera, or any sort of building can have. He knew the lunch wagon had a *phantom*!

Compared to a phantom, a ghost is a joke.

When Gus's Lunch Wagon was still new and the finest thing on West Cheddar Street, people would crowd in to have tuna fish sandwiches and bowls of bean soup. The place was a big success.

But strange things began to happen. Strange stories were told. People said they had heard awful noises coming from the cellar beneath the lunch wagon. People said they had seen long shadows flitting around the lunch wagon at night.

Sometimes, people eating bean soup at the counter heard evil, frightening, scratching noises coming from somewhere above their heads or beneath their feet.

And then...one night...when the lunch wagon was full of people nervously sipping coffee, and nervously eating bean soup, and nervously nibbling tuna fish sandwiches...that night, when the moon was full, and the wind was blowing, and there were no leaves on the trees...and it was cold...the phantom appeared.

Eeeeek!

After that night, no one came back to the lunch wagon. The electric lights burned until the power company turned off the service, and the door blew back and forth on its hinges until someone nailed it shut.

Little by little, people forgot about that terrible night. People forgot about the phantom. Only old Mr. Wiggers remembered, and nobody paid the least attention to him.

And now, Chris Kevin-Keith was making the lunch wagon over, making it brand-new, and he did not know anything about the phantom, and the horrible night so many years ago.

"No good will come of this," old Mr. Wiggers said. "But no one listens to me."

When Chris Kevin-Keith had finished hammering, and sawing, and sanding, and painting, and gluing, and fixing—when he had put in a beautiful new stove, and a beautiful new sink, and a beautiful new refrigerator, he painted a beautiful new sign, and put it on top of the lunch wagon.

THE JOLLY TROLLEY

Chris Kevin-Keith was proud of his lunch wagon. "I love The Jolly Trolley," he said.

Most people loved The Jolly Trolley. When Chris Kevin-Keith opened for business, they all came. They sat on the stools along the counter and had scrambled eggs, cups of coffee, tea, and hot chocolate, and the best toast in town.

"This is just what West Cheddar Street needed," the people all said.

Chris Kevin-Keith had decorated the inside of The Jolly Trolley with models of trolley cars and railroad cars. People loved the decorations.

The Jolly Trolley was busy all night and all day. Everyone ate there, except old Mr. Wiggers.

"I have a bad feeling about this," old Mr. Wiggers said.

One night, some of the people in The Jolly Trolley thought they heard strange noises.

Another night, some people saw strange shadows around The Jolly Trolley. Then some people thought they heard evil, frightening, scratching noises coming from somewhere above their heads or beneath their feet.

People began to talk about the strange things that happened at The Jolly Trolley. They wondered what caused the noises and the shadows.

Then someone found an old, old newspaper. A story told about the phantom at Gus's Lunch Wagon. The next day, there was a brand-new newspaper story. It told that The Jolly Trolley was once Gus's Lunch Wagon. It told about the phantom. And it asked the question: "Is the phantom still there?"

"I could have told them all that," old Mr. Wiggers said. "But nobody listens to me."

After the newspaper story about the phantom, people stopped coming to The Jolly Trolley. Once in a while, someone would peek in a window, but everyone was afraid to go inside. Chris Kevin-Keith sat alone, drinking a cup of hot chocolate and listening to the evil sounds coming from the cellar.

"I am very unhappy," Chris Kevin-Keith said.

Then someone appeared in the doorway. Chris Kevin-Keith looked up from his hot chocolate. Who was it? Could this be...the phantom?

It was old Mr. Wiggers.

"I know I'm probably wasting my time, because nobody listens to me," old Mr. Wiggers said. "But I'd like to talk to you."

Chris Kevin-Keith brought old Mr. Wiggers a cup of hot chocolate. "I've got a phantom," he said.

"I know that," old Mr. Wiggers said.

"I can hear the phantom making evil scratching noises right now," Chris Kevin-Keith said.

"Let's catch it," old Mr. Wiggers said.

"What?" Chris Kevin-Keith exclaimed.

"Nobody! Absolutely nobody listens to me," old Mr. Wiggers said.

"Did you say *catch* the phantom?" Chris Kevin-Keith asked.

"So, you heard me after all," old Mr. Wiggers said.

"But, next to a phantom, a ghost is a joke," Chris Kevin-Keith said.

"I still say catch it. That's what I told Gus."

"You did?"

"Yes, but did he listen to me?"

"If we catch the phantom, it might do bad things to us," Chris Kevin-Keith said.

"If we don't catch the phantom, people will stay away from The Jolly Trolley for years and years," old Mr. Wiggers said.

"You're right," Chris Kevin-Keith said. "We have to catch the phantom, no matter how dangerous it is."

"Where do you think the phantom is right now?" old Mr. Wiggers asked.

"I can hear it making horrible noises in the cellar," Chris Kevin-Keith said. "Listen!"

Old Mr. Wiggers listened. "Yes! I can hear it too! Horrible little moaning noises. Let's go down and catch it."

"Right now?" Chris Kevin-Keith asked.

"Right now," old Mr. Wiggers said. "Do you have a flashlight?"

Chris Kevin-Keith and old Mr. Wiggers went down the steps to the cellar underneath The Jolly Trolley. Chris Kevin-Keith had his flashlight.

"This is too scary," Chris Kevin-Keith said. "Let's leave."

"No," old Mr. Wiggers said. "We have to catch the phantom. Can you hear it?"

"Oh no!" Chris Kevin-Keith said. "I mean, oh yes! I can hear it! I can hear the phantom! It's making a strange rumbling noise. I think it's behind that box!"

"It *is* a strange rumbling noise," old Mr. Wiggers said. "A very quiet sort of noise. Shine your light in that direction."

Chris Kevin-Keith pointed his flashlight at the box, where the strange noise was coming from.t

"Oh no!" Chris Kevin-Keith said. "It's a horrible, scary, evil shadow!"

"I've heard that noise before," old Mr. Wiggers said.

"Oh, this is too scary!" Chris Kevin-Keith said.

"That soft sort of rumbling noise," old Mr. Wiggers said.

"I'm afraid to look!" Chris Kevin-Keith said.

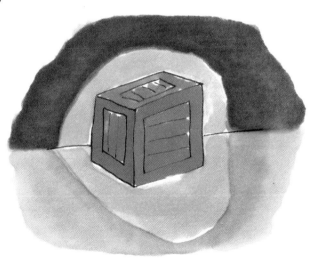

"It sounds like...like purring," old Mr. Wiggers said. "Like the purring of..."

"A kitten!" Chris Kevin-Keith said.

"A kitten!" old Mr. Wiggers said.

"Meow," the kitten said.

It was a very small kitten, white with gray ears.

"That's the phantom? A kitten?" Chris Kevin-Keith asked.

"Some kittens can be awfully fierce," old Mr. Wiggers said.

"That's what's been making horrible noises in the ceiling and under the floor?" Chris Kevin-Keith asked.

"It was a kitten in Gus's day, too," old Mr. Wiggers said.

"That's the phantom?"

"That's the phantom."

The next day there was a story in the newspaper:

LUNCH WAGON OWNER CAPTURES PHANTOM

Chris Kevin-Keith took down the sign that said THE JOLLY TROLLEY, and put up a new one that said:

THE PHANTOM LUNCH WAGON

Soon people came back to the lunch wagon. They sat on the stools along the counter and had scrambled eggs, cups of coffee, tea, and hot chocolate, and the best toast in town.

And sometimes, if they were lucky, the people would hear strange noises coming from the ceiling or the cellar—or they would see strange shadows around the lunch wagon—or they might catch a glimpse of a white kitten with gray ears, drinking milk from a saucer behind the counter.